Accidental Lily

Accidental Lily

by Sally Warner

illustrated by
Jacqueline Rogers

ALFRED A. KNOPF
New York

For Mirja Kivistö

THIS IS A BORZOI BOOK PUBLISHED BY ALFRED A. KNOPF, INC.

Text copyright © 1999 by Sally Warner.
Illustrations copyright © 1999 by Jacqueline Rogers.

All rights reserved under International and Pan-American Copyright
Conventions. Published in the United States of America by
Alfred A. Knopf, Inc., New York, and simultaneously in Canada
by Random House of Canada Limited, Toronto.
Distributed by Random House, Inc., New York.

www.randomhouse.com/kids

Library of Congress Cataloging-in-Publication Data
Warner, Sally.
Accidental Lily / Sally Warner ; illustrated by Jacqueline Rogers.
p.   cm.
Summary: With help from her mother and brother, six-year-old Lily
begins to tackle her bed-wetting problem so that she can go to a sleep-
over party.
ISBN 0-679-89138-2 (trade). — ISBN 0-679-99138-7 (lib. bdg.)
[1. Bedwetting—Fiction. 2. Sleepovers—Fiction.]
I. Rogers, Jacqueline, ill. II. Title.
PZ7.W24644Ac   1999
[Fic]—dc21   98-33883

Printed in the United States of America

10 9 8 7 6 5 4 3 2

CONTENTS

CHAPTER ONE
A Little Accident

"I had another little accident," I say to Mommy. The sun is almost up, I think.

Mommy rolls over in her bed and tries to wrap the pillow around her ears. "Mmph," she says. She hates it when I wet my bed, so she is trying to pretend it didn't happen.

It happened, though. I walk around to the other side of Mommy's bed. "It wasn't my fault," I tell her pillow. "I had a bad dream." I have been having bad dreams ever since we moved to Philadelphia last summer. I never had bad dreams in New Jersey. Not that I remember, anyway.

Mommy opens one of her eyes. "Did you change into clean jammies?" she asks me.

I nod my head.

"Did you go potty?" she asks.

"Two times," I tell her. "Once in my bed, and once in the bathroom. And I'm all shivery out here." Maybe she hasn't noticed.

She sighs and lifts up the covers so I can crawl in next to her. She gives me a kiss on the top of my head. "You smell like a hamster cage," she says.

Hamsters! My favorite, except for their tails. "Thank you," I say, snuggling against her. She smells good, too, like baby powder and leaves.

Mommy giggles. "I meant that you

smell like a hamster cage that needs cleaning," she says. But she gives me one more kiss, so I forgive her.

"Don't tell Case, okay? About my little accident?" I whisper to her. Casey is my big brother. He is twelve, and I am six. I forget how old my mommy is. Old, but she is still pretty.

"Okay," she says, but I can tell she is almost asleep again.

Now I am the one to sigh, because it doesn't matter whether she tells Case I wet my bed or not—he'll know anyway.

How will he know? Not because he is magic, that's for sure. No, he'll know I wet my bed again because of the soggy bundle of sheets next to our apartment's front door.

Mommy will have to run all the way down to the basement and stuff them into the washing machine before we leave for school and work.

And then she will have to put them in the dryer tonight when we get home.

And then she will have to get them out of the dryer after dinner.

And then she will have to make my bed while I am taking a bath.

And then the whole thing will happen all over again.

Probably. It doesn't always happen, though. Some mornings, I wake up as dry as when I went to bed. Drier, if you count my sticky morning eyes and thirsty mouth.

But other mornings, like this one, I

wake up so early that the birds are still asleep, not to mention my mommy and Case. And why do I wake up? Because I have had a little accident, that's why.

Here is what it feels like: Everything seems okay at first. You roll over in your nice cozy bed, and you hear a funny sound. That is because the mattress has plastic all over it so you can't ruin it when you wet the bed. But the plastic makes noise whenever you move. It sounds like you are sleeping inside a sack of potato chips.

And then—all of a sudden—part of you feels cold that shouldn't feel cold.

Oh, no, you think, it has happened again.

You don't want to get up. You try *not*

to get up, but pretty soon you have to, because who wants to lie in a cold, wet bed? When you have cold, wet legs?

Not me, that's who.

You go into the bathroom, even though it is *too late,* and then you peel off your wet jammies and try to find clean ones. You usually stub your toe about now.

If there are no clean jammies in the drawer, you put on an old T-shirt or something. Anything, just so you can go back to bed.

But then you remember—you *can't* go back to bed, because your noisy crackly bed is sopping wet. And anyway, by now you are wide enough awake to count to five hundred by tens.

Which is cinchy—we learned how last year in kindergarten. At my old school.

But it is still dark outside, and you have to do *something*, so you walk over to your mommy's bed and say, "I had another little accident."

At least that's what *I* do.

I would like to know what it feels like to wake up dry every single morning. I would like to wake up dry so many days in a row that I don't even *think* about having a little accident anymore.

I would like to forget I ever had an accident.

If I could only do something about these bad Philadelphia dreams!

CHAPTER TWO
The Reason

"Uh-oh, more laundry," Case says, looking at the ball of sheets next to the front door. We are eating breakfast, but there is no wall between the kitchen and the living room in this apartment.

"Shut up," I tell him, but soft, so Mommy can't hear. She is standing at the counter, making our lunches. She says it is rude and vulgar to tell other people to shut up.

"You shut up," Case says under his breath.

"No, you," I say. "And anyway, I can't help it if I had a little accident," I say. "I had another bad dream." I pour some

8

more cereal into my bowl. Waking up in the middle of the night makes you hungry!

"What was it about?" Case asks.

I chew my cereal and think, hard. What was it about? That's a good question.

I think this is what nightmares *should* be about:

1. Monsters.

2. Bad guys.

3. The dark.

But if you follow the rules I figured out, you should not have bad dreams about these three things! Here are the rules:

1. Do not watch scary TV shows or movies about monsters, and you will not have nightmares about monsters. Also, do not let your big brother pretend that he is a monster. Yell for Mommy if he does.

2. Do not watch the news or TV shows about the highway patrol, and you will not dream about bad guys. If you see one of those shows by mistake, yell for Mommy.

3. Have night-lights in every single room, and you will not have bad dreams about the dark. If one of the lights burns out, yell for Mommy.

It is that simple—or it should be.

The trouble is, my Philadelphia nightmares are not about monsters, or bad guys, or the dark.

They are about flying, which should be a *good* dream, in my opinion.

My flying dreams start out fine. Sometimes I am at our old house in New Jersey. A scary, shadowy person comes in the front door, and I have to fly out the back door to escape! Only something always goes wrong—like my wings don't work.

Sometimes I am in our new apartment when I have to fly. Well, it's not new, and it's not really an apartment. We rent the top half of an old house from Buddy Haynes, who lives downstairs with his beautiful dog, Champion. It is very strange living in someone else's house, I think.

But in my bad dreams, Buddy is not there to guard the stairs when the nightmare-person comes into the building, and Champion is not there to bark. I am there, but I am upstairs. I hear the person coming up the stairs, *clomp, clomp, clomp,* and I know I have to fly out the window. When I do, though, I can't stay up in the air!

No wonder I wet my bed! You would, too. You'd wet *your* bed, I mean.

Case is still waiting to hear what my bad dream was about.

"I don't remember," I tell him.

"Well, it doesn't even matter," Case says, "because that's not the reason you wet your bed."

"Case," Mommy says from where she is standing, next to the sink. "Stay out of this, please."

"What do you mean that's not the reason?" I ask him, my voice a little screechy. Case thinks he knows everything! And he doesn't. He doesn't!

Case shrugs. "I mean just what I said," he tells me. "Your bad dream is not the reason you wet the bed."

"What *is* the reason, if you know so much?" I ask him.

"Case," my mommy says again, like she is warning him about a cartoon piano that is about to fall on his stupid head.

Case looks at Mommy, then he clamps his mouth shut. He pulls his fingers across the front of his lips, like he is locking them.

Now he decides to listen to Mommy. No fair!

Case shoves his chair back and carries his dishes to the sink. Mommy goes to the front door, grabs the dirty sheets, and goes down to the basement.

And I get a bright idea. Before Case can go brush his teeth, I jump up from the table, run into the bathroom, and slam the door shut behind me. I'm not opening it again, either, not until Casey leaves to catch the bus. And he knows it, too.

Hah! My big brother will have to go to Ben Franklin Middle School with dirty teeth today. It serves him right! Too bad we didn't have spinach for breakfast, or candied apples. He'd be in big trouble then.

I spend a long time in front of the bathroom mirror, brushing my hair. It is only brown, like a mouse's hair. My new friend Daisy Greenough has shiny yellow hair. LaVon Hamilton, my other new friend, has black hair, three braids, and barrettes that match every single outfit she wears. No fair.

Finally, Mommy knocks on the bath-room door. "It's time to leave for school, Lily," she says.

"Okay," I say, opening the door. I pick up my backpack and smile at Mommy. I pretend that nothing bad happened last night or this morning.

Sometimes that works.

Not today, though. When Mommy and I are about to cross the street, which means that we are halfway to Betsy Ross Primary School, she says, "Casey was only trying to help, sweetie-pie."

I try to tug my hand away from hers, but that is not allowed when we are crossing busy city streets. She holds on tight. "Sure," I say, but in a secret way that really means *Are you crazy? He was not!*

"He's your brother, Lily. He cares about you."

"Huh," I say. "Case thinks I wet my bed on purpose."

"No he doesn't," Mommy says. "Be fair—he never said that, and I know he doesn't *think* that."

"Then what *does* he think?" I ask Mommy. We have finished crossing the street, but we are still holding hands.

"He thinks you drink too much water before bedtime," Mommy says.

Now I yank my hand away. "I do not," I say. "I hardly drink any water before I go to bed. Only a little, when I brush my teeth." I am not really sure this is true, but I don't like my big brother and my mommy talking about me behind my back.

"Well, that's his theory," Mommy says.

Oh, great, I think. So Case has a whole theory about me! He has been spying, watching how much water I drink every night. It's not like he's so perfect!

"It's none of his beeswax," I say, copying Stevie, who is in my class at school. "And anyway, it's not the water that causes the accidents—it's those nightmares, and they happen because we moved to Philadelphia."

I sneak a look at Mommy when I say this. She doesn't like to hear me complain about moving to the city. She says we didn't have a choice.

Sure enough, her mouth is scrunching up and her eyebrows are scrunching down. "Your bad dreams are all about Philadelphia?" she asks me.

"Well, no," I say, trying to be fair. "But I never had the dreams until we moved here."

Mommy sighs. "I'm sorry you're still so upset about the move, sweetie," she says. "But you know, things are going to get better for you. And for us all."

"When?" I ask her. "When I'm *old*? When I'm a teenager?"

Mommy laughs. "No—before that, I promise," she says. "Listen, you're starting to make friends already, aren't you?"

"I guess," I say, my voice grumbly.

Mommy raises her hand like she is making a promise. "Things will settle down, and then I think you'll find that the bed-wetting will stop," she tells me.

"That's easy for you to say," I mumble. "You're not the one with cold, wet legs all the time."

Mommy opens her mouth to answer me, but we are almost at the steps of my school. Kids are running every which way and yelling. Some big fifth graders are chasing each other around, and even eating their lunches already! It is hard to talk, and harder to listen.

All of a sudden, I see LaVon come skipping through the crowds of kids like they aren't even there. She is the best skipper! "Hi," she says when she reaches us. She gives a shy smile to my mommy.

"Hello, LaVon," Mommy says. "Don't you look cute today!"

LaVon gives a real smile now and holds

out her lime-green skirt. She is wearing a polka-dot top that matches perfectly. So do her barrettes, of course. But I don't ever hate LaVon, because she is so nice.

"We'd better go or we'll be late," LaVon says to me. "Bye, Mrs. Hill," she tells my mommy.

"Bye, girls," Mommy says. She looks at me with hungry eyes, like she would like to say something more. It is too crowded, though, and there is no time.

And I am glad our conversation is over.

After all, I think, no matter what she says, this is all her fault.

She's the one who made us move.

CHAPTER THREE
Friends

I am in the first grade, and my teacher's name is Ms. Marshall. Me and Daisy and LaVon took a vote and decided that Ms. Marshall is pretty, but not beautiful. I wanted her to be beautiful because she has mouse-brown hair, like me, but Daisy and LaVon said no way.

Ms. Marshall pulls her hair back in a kind of braid, but it is always coming loose. She is wearing pink lipstick this morning, maybe because it is a brand-new day. She is a hopeful person. She has probably forgotten what a terrible day she had yesterday! She had to do her yoga breathing seven times. I counted.

But her lipstick will be all gone by the time we have nutrition break, and that is way before lunch. I guess she chews it off. I wonder what lipstick tastes like? Someday I will find out.

I think that maybe this is the first year Ms. Marshall has taught at Betsy Ross Primary School. It's the first year she's taught *me*, anyway!

Today, the wind starts blowing hard outside when we are in the middle of doing our numbers. I am trying to make my sevens pointy enough, like kitty ears. Last time we did sevens, some of mine were kind of droopy.

Marcus, the terrible boy who sits next

to me in class, makes perfect sevens. And eights. And nines. He barely even tries, either! He could probably do a whole row of sevens standing on his head, but not me. I have to stick my tongue out a little and hold my pencil so tight when I work that my fingers get lines in them. No fair.

Marcus and Stevie Braddock are best friends. Stevie's this other bad boy in my class. School has only been going for six weeks, but already Ms. Marshall knows enough to make Stevie sit as far away from Marcus as possible without putting him in the hall.

Me and Daisy and LaVon would vote for putting him in the hall, if we could.

So Marcus misses Stevie, and he takes it out on me. "What's the matter, can't you do

sevens?" he asks, his voice whispery so Ms. Marshall doesn't hear him. It is the kind of question that doesn't really want an answer. He holds out his worksheet, admiring it in a fakey way.

"I can do sevens fine," I mutter at him, and I crunch my teeth together to keep from saying rude and vulgar words. *Seven, seven, seven,* I think. I have been pressing down so hard on my pencil that the point is gone. I hate making pointy numbers with a worn-out pencil.

I raise my hand and wave it back and forth. Maybe Ms. Marshall will let me go sharpen my pencil! You have to ask permission, though.

She is helping Hilary, this shy girl by the

window. She doesn't see me, so I shake my arm harder to get her attention.

And then that stupid Marcus does a trick that he and Stevie Braddock just love. Marcus knocks on his desk, hard, and flops over at the same time, pretending he has been hit—by *me,* waving my arm. "Ow!" he says, real loud. He puts his hand on his mouth, like that's where it hurts.

Now I have Ms. Marshall's attention. Oh, great. "Lily Hill, are you bothering your neighbor?" she asks from across the room.

Marcus is smiling, but Ms. Marshall is too far away to see it. Stevie stands up to get a better look at us. His face almost falls off, he is laughing so hard.

Me, bothering my neighbor! That's what

I used to get in trouble for all the time at my old school, when I was in kindergarten. But I never meant to bother anyone. It just came naturally to me then.

I wouldn't mind bothering my neighbor now, though! But only if I could do it secretly, without getting into any trouble. I would like to pound Marcus good! I won't, though, because Marcus and Stevie are the boy bosses of the class. I try to stay out of their way.

"No, I am not bothering my neighbor," I tell Ms. Marshall, very brave. "I just need to sharpen my pencil, that's all. That's why I raised my hand," I say, so she will know that I followed her rules.

"Well, all right," Ms. Marshall says, "but be a little more careful next time, Lily.

We're awfully crowded in here. I don't want anyone getting hurt."

And all I was trying to do was make sharp, pointy sevens! I was doing it for *her*. "Okay," I mumble. LaVon turns around in her seat and sticks her tongue out at Marcus, but that just makes him happier.

This has been a perfect morning for Marcus, and do you know what? He doesn't even hate me! That's the weird part. He's been almost-nice to me during recess the last couple of weeks. I guess goofing around is just something he does when he finishes his worksheets early, which is most of the time. Goofing around is kind of like his job.

Marcus is smiling big now.

"Thanks a lot," I whisper, getting up to sharpen my stupid pencil.

"You're welcome a lot," he says, pretending to be polite.

Just when it is my turn at the pencil sharpener, the bell rings for nutrition break, which is also recess. I am almost trampled by hungry kids running to the cloakroom for their snacks. "Line up, everyone," Ms. Marshall says in a croaky voice.

In the cloakroom, Stevie and Marcus take turns shoving me. Just a little bit, so it doesn't hurt. But Stevie says, "Ow" when he pushes me, like I'm the one who bumped into *him*, and then Marcus says it, too. I guess that will be their big joke for the next hundred years.

LaVon says, "Quit it! You guys are so

lame." They pretend not to listen to her, but they stop shoving. LaVon is the girl boss of the class.

We get out our snacks while Ms. Marshall is still trying to line everyone up. I have peanut butter graham crackers today, and LaVon has a biscuit with some ham in the middle. My mouth gets watery when I look at it.

Poor Daisy has carrots, and they aren't nice skinny strips, either. Just plain, bare carrots, not even peeled, with a white carrot whisker on the end of each one. Yick.

Daisy's mom believes in food that is a little too healthy. Even Daisy thinks so. She doesn't say anything, but you can tell. LaVon and I bring extra snacks, though, so Daisy doesn't starve. She is our friend!

"Want some carrot?" Daisy asks when we reach the yard, which is full of wind and yelling kids. LaVon has already started skipping, but she will come back to us pretty soon. Her skirt looks like a little green kite blowing across the playground.

"No, thank you," I say. "But here, have a graham cracker sandwich."

"Oh, okay," Daisy says, like it is no big deal—like she is not practically starving. She starts chomping away. We walk over to the bench.

"I want to ask you a question," I say. "Do you know a way to stop having bad dreams?"

Daisy licks graham cracker crumbs from her lips and hugs her jacket tight around her. She frowns, thinking hard. "I used to get them all the time when I was little," she says. "I used to dream there was this terrible—"

"Don't tell me!" I say, covering up my ears fast. "That's all I need, another scary thing to dream about!"

Daisy giggles, and her yellow bangs blow in the wind. "Sorry," she says.

"But how did you stop having the dreams?" I ask. "That's what I want to know."

Daisy thinks for a minute. "Well, I was sleeping on my stomach whenever a nightmare woke me up," she says, like that's the answer.

"So?"

"So that's the thing," Daisy says, as if she

is on a TV show and has just explained what is behind curtain number three. "You have to sleep on your back!"

"All night long?" I ask her. I am trying to figure out how you could do that. How can you be the boss of your nighttime self?

Daisy nods, and her bangs bounce. "Yup," she says. "It's easy." She looks at the little plastic bag I am holding.

I hand her another graham cracker sandwich. "Okay, how?" I ask.

Crunch, crunch, crunch. "Well," she finally says, "you lie on your back when it's time to go to bed, and then you do two things. First you cross your ankles, and then you put your hands under your head. That way, you can't roll over onto your stomach—even in your sleep."

I frown. This is confusing! "I don't get it," I say. "My hands go under my head?"

Daisy clasps her fingers together and puts them behind her head. Her elbows come up like wings. "You know," she says, "kind of like you do on the Fourth of July? When you are lying on the grass at Fairmount Park, watching fireworks?"

She forgets that I just moved to Philadelphia, but I am excited now. "On the Fourth of July, I am blowing out birthday candles!" I tell Daisy.

"Lucky!" Daisy says, just as LaVon comes skipping up to us.

"Who's lucky?" LaVon asks.

"Lily is. She gets to have a birthday on the Fourth of July," Daisy says.

LaVon smiles big. "Well, *my* birthday's

November first," she says, and then she waits, like she is expecting us to congratulate her.

I am thinking, *November first? What's so great about that?*

"You know," LaVon says with a laugh, "the day after Halloween! And that's not all," she says, wiggling onto the bench in between me and Daisy. "Guess what?" she asks. She hands Daisy a hunk of her ham biscuit, and my stomach gurgles again, just from the idea of it. My stomach has a good imagination.

"Mmm," Daisy says, biting into the biscuit. "What?"

"Halloween is on a Saturday this year," LaVon says. "That hardly ever happens. It means that I get to go trick-or-treating with friends, and then have a sleep-over party, if I want!"

My heart starts to go *ka-thunk* inside my jacket. This sounds like the most fun party I have ever heard about! Trick-or-treating, and then—hey, wait a minute, I think. A sleep-over? I have never been to one of those.

"And guess who I'm inviting?" LaVon asks, her voice all teasy.

"Me!" Daisy yells, jumping up from the bench. Her bag of hairy carrots bounces to the ground.

"And me, too?" I ask LaVon, getting up more slowly. Ms. Marshall got a whistle last week, and now she is blowing it, hard. That means we have had enough nutrition. It is time to go back to class and work on our words.

"Of *course* you are invited, too," LaVon says, giving me a little shove. Her lime-green barrettes twinkle in the sunlight. "It'll be so much fun," she says. "We can eat our trick-or-treat candy and talk real late. Who knows when we'll fall asleep?"

Ka-thunk! goes my heart again as we are lining up.

Fall asleep?

In somebody else's house?

In somebody else's room?

In somebody else's bed?

Which I will probably wet?

No way!

This will be the best party invitation I have ever gotten in my whole life so far, and I will have to just say no.

Unless Daisy's goofy plan works, that is.

CHAPTER FOUR
Family Stuff

"Okay, now tuck me in real tight," I tell Mommy when it is time to go to bed. My ankles are crossed, and my hands are behind my head. There is no way that I am going to roll over onto my stomach tonight! I don't tell Mommy my plan, though, because I don't want to get her hopes up too high.

"Is this tight enough?" Mommy asks me. You can barely even see my legs anymore, they are smooshed down so flat.

"That's good," I say. "Now give me a kiss good night, okay? I can't move."

Mommy smoothes my hair back and kisses me on the forehead. "Did you go potty, sweetie?" she asks me. A serious look is on her face.

I nod my head. I didn't *only* go potty before bedtime, though, and I don't *only* have my ankles crossed and my hands behind my head so I can't roll over in the middle of the night, either. I did some other secret tricks to keep from wetting my bed, too:

1. I kissed all my stuffed animals and dolls twice, for luck. But I only kissed the ones I brought with me from my old house in New Jersey, where I never wet my bed. Well, hardly ever.

2. I wore underpants underneath my jammies. Maybe I can trick my nighttime

self into thinking I am in school, and not in bed!

3. I drank only half a glass of water in the bathroom after I brushed my teeth, not a whole glass. Maybe Case is half-right about drinking water before bedtime. I'm not going to tell *him* that, though!

It didn't work.

I don't remember having a bad flying dream, exactly, but I must have had one.

When I wake up, it is still dark out. Even though I am still lying on my back, all the covers are untucked, my pillow is on the floor—and my legs are cold and wet.

So I go into the bathroom, change my

jammies, stub my toe, and tell my sleepy mommy, "Sorry, but I had another little accident."

It's kind of nice to cuddle up with Mommy so early in the morning.

At breakfast, Case looks over at the pile of laundry by the door, but today he doesn't say a thing. He and Mommy look at each other, though, and Case's eyes say *Poor you* to her.

"Shut up," I whisper to him. I try to kick his leg under the kitchen table, but I hit the table leg instead. "Ow," I say.

"Lily's kicking," Case says, like he's reporting the weather.

Mommy is reading the newspaper again. "Don't kick," she says, not looking up.

"I have to," I say. "There's a fly on my foot. It's bothering me." I make a face at my brother.

Case gets up from the table. "I have to leave early," he says. "I'm meeting Ned at the bus stop in ten minutes."

Ned! He is Casey's new best friend in Philadelphia. I like him much better than I like Case most of the time. Sometimes, I wish I could trade—Case for Ned. Ned lives with his grandmother, and he doesn't have any little brothers or sisters. When he comes over, Ned listens to every single word I have to say.

Hey, wait a minute, I think—what if Case tells Ned that I wet my bed? I don't want Ned thinking I am a baby. "Uh, Casey?" I say, trying to sound extra nice.

Case is running around the apartment. He is grabbing his lunch, stuffing his notebook into his backpack, and brushing his teeth, all at the same time.

"Mmm?" he says, his red toothbrush sticking out of his mouth.

I try to think of what words to say while he runs to rinse out his mouth in the bathroom. I have to think quick, though, because he is about to leave. "Um, some of our family stuff is private, okay?" I finally say.

"You mean about Dad being gone?" he says, putting on his jacket. "Ned already knows all about Dad—I told him the whole story," he says. Case's face looks empty now, like somebody has just erased the blackboard.

Mommy doesn't say a word, but she is listening, hard. She puts a finger on the newspaper to save her place.

"I didn't mean about Daddy," I say. "I was talking about *that*." I look at the bundle of soggy sheets.

Case looks confused for a moment. "You mean...No," he says, his face filling up again. "I'm not going to tell Ned you wet your bed every night. Why should I? It's not that interesting, believe me."

"I don't wet my bed *every* night!" I yell.

"Okay, whatever," Case says, picking up his backpack. "See ya." And he is gone.

"I don't," I say, turning to Mommy.

"I know, honey," she says. "Not every night."

"And I'm trying to change," I tell her. "Anyway, I'm the one who has to suffer," I say, thinking of LaVon's birthday sleepover—which I will not get to go to, all because of you-know-what. I am a girl who will go to no parties!

Mommy looks at the dirty sheets and sighs. "We all suffer a little, Lily," she says.

"Well, not Case," I say. "And he'd better not tell Ned I wet my bed, that's all I have to say."

"That's really all you have to say?" Mommy asks me, getting up. She is smiling now.

"Well, yeah," I say. "For now. Until I think of something else, anyway!"

CHAPTER FIVE
The Fight

Uh-oh, Marcus and Stevie are having a fight. I can tell as soon as I walk into the cloakroom to hang up my jacket.

I don't know what it is about, and I don't know who started it, but Marcus is winning. "Oof," Stevie says as Marcus pushes him into the wall, accidentally-on-purpose.

"Sorry, *Stevie*," Marcus says. He is looking around secretly to see if anyone is watching. He wants us kids to watch, but not Ms. Marshall. She says that she has eyes in the back of her head, but that's not true. She misses a lot.

She is missing this.

"Well, quit it," Stevie says, brushing off his arm like it has gotten germs from the wall.

"Yeah, quit it," LaVon says. She is hanging up her backpack, which is the best one in the class. It is fuzzy and shaped like a bear. It even has paws! I want one just like it for Christmas, but I don't want LaVon to think I am copying.

I will worry about that later, though. Right now, I am just trying to watch this fight without getting hit.

"You'll be sorry," Stevie says to Marcus.

"Oh, yeah? When?" Marcus asks, laughing a little bit.

Stevie frowns. "When I tell everybody that you *wet your bed*," he says—loud, so that everyone can hear.

Everyone hears, all right, but nobody says a word.

All of a sudden, Marcus's face doesn't have any expression on it at all. He doesn't say a word. He just stares at Stevie.

"Well, it's true," Stevie says, turning to us like we are arguing with him. "I slept over at his house, and that's what happened. He wet his bed, just like a baby."

"I did not," Marcus finally says. "And anyway, you sucked your thumb!" But nobody believes Marcus about the thumb—he's just trying to get even. He is standing there like a big plastic Marcus-doll, and only his mouth is moving. He doesn't look real, almost, and so his words don't sound real, either.

I think Marcus *does* wet his bed—just like me!

Daisy giggles, but it sounds like she really is about to cry instead. I poke her with my elbow, and she stops.

We hear Ms. Marshall clapping her hands for us to come sit down, and everyone in the cloakroom marches into class like we are in a very sad parade. We take our seats.

Some of the cloakroom kids start whispering right away in their seats, telling their neighbors this exciting news. The room is filling up with a buzzy sound, all except for me and Marcus and—way across the room—Stevie Braddock.

Stevie's face has started to look pinchy and sad. I'll bet he wishes he never opened his big fat mouth. After all, Marcus is his best friend! Or he used

to be. Pushing and shoving is one thing, but telling secrets about your friends is something else.

Stevie probably wishes he could grab those bed-wetting words and throw them away, but he can't. They already jumped right inside everyone's ears.

Marcus is looking straight ahead at nothing.

I am looking sideways at Marcus.

Ms. Marshall is looking confused. "Okay, girls and boys," she says, "simmer down. What's gotten into you today?"

Nobody raises their hand to answer her, so she takes a deep yoga breath and passes out our worksheets.

We are supposed to sharpen our pencils before class starts, but I was too busy watching the fight in the cloak-room. This means I am going to have to draw a whole page of eights with a worn-out pencil. I give a big sigh.

"Here," Marcus says. He pushes a brand-new, very sharp pencil my way.

I jump a little in my seat, because he has surprised me. "Thanks," I whisper.

We draw eights for a while. I am getting better at them, *finally*.

As usual, Marcus fills his page before everybody else, but today he doesn't goof around when he is done. Instead, he stares down at his desk and taps his pencil against his hand.

The pencil moves so fast that it is almost a blur.

I can't stop watching it.

Suddenly, a big hand touches my shoulder. *"Yahhh!"* I shout, jumping about a mile.

It is only Ms. Marshall! Everybody laughs. Even Ms. Marshall, even Marcus. I can feel my cheeks getting hot. "Back to work, everyone," Ms. Marshall finally says. She leans over and whispers, "Good work on those eights, Lily. But try to finish the whole page today."

Finally, it is time for nutrition break. Those eights have made me hungry! I go sharpen Marcus's pencil, and my pencil, too. Marcus is still sitting at his desk, pretending to be busy. "Here," I say, and I hand him the pencil.

He scowls at me, so I hurry away.

By the time I get to the playground, LaVon is almost jumping up and down, she is so excited. Daisy is busy peeking into her snack bag. She has granola today, but not the fun kind.

"What took you?" LaVon asks me.

"Pencil sharpener," I say. I am getting to be famous in class for having problems with my pencils. I would rather be famous for something else—like being the best skipper, or being the smartest. Or for being the cutest!

I wouldn't want to be famous for being the kid who still wets her bed, though. I think about Marcus, and I feel sad for him. I even feel sorry for Stevie Braddock. He is famous now for saying bad things about his best friend.

Stevie is all by himself, kicking a ball against the fence.

Marcus is sitting on the bench, eating his snack. He is alone, too.

LaVon hands me an orange piece of paper. "What's this?" I ask her.

"It's your invitation," she says. She looks around, pretending to be nervous. We are not supposed to pass out birthday party invitations at school unless we are going to invite everybody.

But no one is watching us. "Go ahead, open it," LaVon says, touching the invitation one last time. She made it herself, I can tell. There is about a ton of glitter on the front! LaVon has such cool stuff.

Inside the card, LaVon's mother has printed some words and numbers. "Huh," I say, trying to look happy.

"LaVon told me what it says," Daisy

announces, sounding important. "It says *Please come to a birthday sleep-over at LaVon's house on Halloween night*," she recites, like she is saying the Pledge of Allegiance.

Oh, no, I think—*this party is really going to happen.*

"We can all go trick-or-treating together first," LaVon says, very excited. "Hey, maybe your big brother can take us!" The only thing in the world that LaVon doesn't have is a big brother. For some reason, she thinks she is missing something.

"Maybe. I could ask," I say. "But—but I have to check with my mommy first, to see if I can even come to your sleep-over. She might say no," I tell LaVon.

And Mommy had <u>better</u> say no, I

think. Otherwise I will end up just like Marcus, with everyone saying what a baby I am for wetting my bed. After LaVon and Daisy tell them all about it, that is.

A hurt look pops into LaVon's eyes. "But you have to come," she says. "I'm just asking my two best friends, you and Daisy. It's all planned!"

"Well, but I still have to check," I say. I try to look like a girl whose mommy is very, very strict. "I don't know if I'll be allowed to do it or not."

"How about if LaVon's mom calls your mom?" Daisy asks me. Daisy's mother is Mrs. Greenough, and she is a very bossy lady. She is always picking up the phone and calling everyone to tell them what to do. That's why Daisy thought up this plan.

"That would only make things worse," I tell them both. "*I'll* ask her," I say.

Next to the gate, Ms. Marshall is blowing her silver whistle. It is time to line up and walk back to class.

I am the second person in line, right behind Marcus. I have hidden LaVon's invitation under my jacket.

But feeling the lumpy invitation and seeing gloomy Marcus gives me an idea.

When I get back to the cloakroom, I sneak the invitation into my backpack. But first, I tear one corner off it.

At my desk, I take my nice sharp pencil and write a secret message on the scrap of orange construction paper. Then I put it on Marcus's seat, just before he gets there.

But—oh, no! He starts to sit down without even seeing it.

Marcus has to see it! Otherwise, maybe he will go through the rest of the day with my secret message stuck to his behind.

Then kids will laugh even harder at him, and he will feel even sadder.

"Pssst," I say to him, just before he sits down. *This stupid plan is not working out,* I think. And I was just trying to be nice!

"Huh?" Marcus says.

I bite my lip and point down to the tiny folded orange note.

Marcus scoops it up, unfolds it, and reads it.

I already know what it says, of course. On the note, I have written: me 2.

This is to let him know that he is not the only person in the world who wets his bed. Only I didn't want him to know who sent it!

Marcus flops down in his seat and grins at me. He is starting to look a little like the old Marcus again, the one who says, "Ow" whenever he shoves me. "You too?" he asks, quiet for once.

I try to look casual—and very, very dry. "Sometimes," I whisper. "When I have a bad dream. But don't tell anyone, okay?"

"Okay," Marcus says. And then the funniest thing happens! He digs around in his pocket and comes up with a fluffy little pile of folded notes. There are four of them!

He unfolds them one at a time under his desk and shows them to me. They say:

I dont care

Stevie Stinks.

So do I.

so what?

I start to get the giggles. This is so cool—four other kids have passed Marcus secret notes! "Stevie Braddock *does* stink," I whisper to Marcus.

"Maybe, maybe not," Marcus says.

"Maybe not?" I ask him. If it was me Stevie had told about, I wouldn't be so nice.

In fact, I would feel so embarrassed that I would want to change schools.

But Marcus shrugs his shoulders. "He's probably sorry by now," he says.

"Huh," I say.

And then Ms. Marshall passes out the new worksheets, so there is no more time to think.

CHAPTER SIX
Lily Is Scared!

"Where in the world did all this glitter come from?" Mommy asks, looking at the floor next to the kitchen table. She lifts up one of her feet like the glitter is a nasty sidewalk-thing she has stepped on.

"I got an invitation," I say, sounding gloomy. "Here." I hand the orange invitation to LaVon's party to my mommy. Some more hunks of glitter fall to the floor.

"Oh, for heaven's sake," Mommy says, cranky. "What a mess! Now I'm going to have to get out the vacuum cleaner."

"Mommy, it's *art*," I explain to her.

64

"LaVon made an invitation for me and one for Daisy. But I don't want to go to her stupid party."

"Let's see," Case says, and he looks at the design LaVon made. "Pretty good," he says. Case is an artist, so he should know.

But Mommy holds the invitation carefully, like it is a grouchy turtle that might snap at her. She opens it up and reads what is inside. Then she looks at me, confused. "Well, Lily, this sounds like fun! And I know you like LaVon," she says. "So why don't you want to go to her party?"

"It's a *sleep-over*," I say.

Mommy is still confused. "Lily, I know it's pretty exciting when you sleep away from home for the very first

time, but there's nothing to be nervous about. I've met Mrs. Hamilton, sweetie. She's very nice."

Mrs. Hamilton is LaVon's mother. And sure, she's nice *now*—but what about after I ruin one of her beds? No way will the mattresses at her house have crinkly plastic wrapped all around them, to save them from me.

And who am I supposed to crawl in bed with in the middle of the night?

I can just see it: *I go creeping into Mrs. Hamilton's bedroom in the dark. "Mrs. Hamilton," I say, "I had a little accident in the other room."*

"A little accident?" she asks, and then I have to explain.

"That means I wet the bed," I say to her.

"Oh, nooo!" she screams, and every light in LaVon's house goes on.

The night would be a disaster, that's all.

LaVon will hate me for wrecking her party. And she or Daisy might tell everyone at school what happened!

So I give my mommy a look. "Mrs. Hamilton is not *that* nice," I say.

"Lily is scared!" Case says. "She's afraid she'll wet the bed while she's at LaVon's house." He is talking like he is a magic mind reader or something. Oh, sure, he is right *this* time, but lots of times he is wrong!

"Shut up," I tell him, and I make a face. "This is just between me and Mommy."

Mommy is opening cans now, and

some chopped-up onion is spittering in a big flat pan on the stove. Oh, boy, spaghetti sauce!

"Is that what you're afraid of, Lily?" Mommy asks over her shoulder.

"Kinda," I say, and I make another face at Casey. He shrugs, laughs, and flops down in the big telephone chair with a book he is reading. Dust speckles fly up from the old blue and green cushions.

Case is sitting right where he can hear me and Mommy. Oh, great.

"But it would be a shame for you to miss that party," Mommy says, chopping up a pink square of hamburger meat in the pan with her spatula.

Case looks up from his book. "And it would be fun for us, Mom," he says, grinning. "It would get Lily out of the house for a night. I could use a break."

"Well, even if I went, you wouldn't get a break from me," I tell him, "because LaVon wants you to take us out trick-or-treating before the sleep-over. Hey," I say, thinking fast, "maybe I could do the trick-or-treating part, but not the sleep-over!"

Case shrugs. "I'd consider going with you guys," he says, "if Ned could come, too. We're not doing anything else—and it might be kind of fun! In a weird way."

"I think you should say yes to the whole thing, Lily," Mommy tells me. "It'll be your first party since we moved to the city."

"And it would be my *last* party, too," I say to her. Right now I am so mad that I would run into the bathroom and slam the door behind me—except the spaghetti sauce smells so good!

"Hmm," Mommy says. She is either thinking of what to say next, or she is trying to figure out how many spaghetti sticks to throw into the big pot of boiling water. We always end up with a big old knot of cold noodles, though, no matter how much she tries to plan.

"Pssst," Case says to me while Mommy is thinking. He waves his hand like he wants me to come over to the big squashy chair.

I walk over real slow. "What?" I say.

"I figured out a way for you to go to the party," he says. "Part of a way, I mean. But you'll have to figure out the rest."

"Well, what did you figure out?" I say.

I draw my finger around one of the blue flowers on the chair.

"We find you a sleeping bag," Case announces. "You know, one of those ones you can use indoors. The kind you can put in the washing machine if—if it gets dirty. Ned has one! It's real old, but it's still good."

"Ned wets his *bed?*" I ask. I can't believe it. Ned is almost thirteen!

"No, he doesn't wet his bed," Case says, sounding mad. "Sleeping bags are not just for people who wet their beds, Lily."

"Well, *duh,*" I say, like I have known this all along.

"Hey," Case says, excited now, "maybe Ned would even lend his sleeping bag to you for the party!"

"I don't think that's such a great idea," I say.

"Why not?" Case asks.

"Because then you would have to explain to him about—about everything," I say. "You know, our private family stuff."

Case frowns. "You mean I'd have to tell him that you wet the bed?" he asks.

"Yeah," I say, "and you promised that you wouldn't." My voice sounds creaky when I say this.

"But Mom could wash the sleeping bag after the party!" Case says. "In fact, I know she would wash it just to be polite, whether you had a little accident or not. Which you won't, if you remember what I told you about drinking water before you go to bed."

"Do you mean *any* water?" I ask him.

"Any water," Case says. He sounds very strict now, the way Ms. Marshall does when we have worn her to a frazzle.

Mommy is carrying the spaghetti to the kitchen table. "What are you two whispering about over there?"

"I'm telling Lily a story," Case says, joking. He looks at his book. "And this little piggy went wee-wee-wee-wee, all the way home!" he says, pretending to read.

"Case!" I yell. I do not like wee-wee jokes.

"Okay," Case says, and he turns the page. "How about this story, then? It's called *Water, Water Everywhere,* by I. P. Freely."

I. P. Free—oh, I get it! I pee freely!

"Case, quit it," I say, but I am giggling just a little bit.

"Casey, that joke was old when *I* was in school," Mommy says. "Now go wash your hands, you two."

"I pee freely," I say to Case in the bathroom. The soap jumps out of my hands, and he grabs it.

"No, *I* pee freely," he says, bumping into me with his hip.

"No, I do," I say, bumping him.

"Okay, you win," he says.

I win!

"But here's what you still have to figure out about LaVon's birthday party," Case says while we are drying our hands.

"What?" I ask him.

"You have to make it so it's no big deal if you bring a sleeping bag," he says.

"Yeah," I say. Now I am worried. "Maybe LaVon won't let me bring one. Maybe Mrs. Hamilton has special fancy beds for me and Daisy!"

"She probably doesn't," Case says. "But you'd better make sure."

At dinner, Mommy cuts up my spaghetti so I can eat it neater, but Case slurps his up like that dog in *Lady and the Tramp*. Mommy gets him his own roll of paper towels. "So what about LaVon's party?" she asks me. "I should call Mrs. Hamilton tonight, don't you think?"

"Nuh-uh," I say, shaking my head. Some spaghetti sauce flies off, and Casey hands me one of his paper towels.

"Was that a *no?*" Mommy asks, tilting her head.

"Yes," I say. "I mean, no. I mean, yes, it was a *no*. I want to talk to LaVon about something first."

"She wants to ask LaVon a question," Case says. He is trying to be helpful, but I can do this myself! I give him a look, and he goes back to his spaghetti.

"Well, okay," Mommy says slowly, "but we really do have to call by tomorrow night. So can you talk to LaVon tomorrow, Lily?"

I nod my head *yes*.

Nodding is an easy thing to do, because you don't use any words. But tomorrow, when I talk to LaVon, words are what I am going to need.

Uh-oh!

CHAPTER SEVEN
Skipping

Guess what? I think my plan worked!

Okay, okay, so part of it was Case's idea. But I'm the one who had to talk to LaVon at nutrition break.

She said that sleeping bags were a good idea. She said it would be more like a real slumber party that way.

Daisy says she has a sleeping bag, too, so that's good.

Phew!

Marcus is sitting next to me just like nothing happened yesterday. I thought maybe he would stay home with a sore throat or a stomach ache, or something, but no. He is brave! Maybe he is a little bit quieter than usual, though.

Stevie is pretending nothing happened yesterday, too, but kids aren't playing with him very much today. Who wants a friend who blabs about all your most embarrassing stuff?

But during recess, Marcus kicks a ball, and it zigzags off the fence. Stevie kicks it back and yells, "Think fast!"

Marcus smiles at him kind of crooked. "I think faster than you, anyway," he says, swiping his foot at the ball. Lots of kids are watching them by now.

"Yeah," Stevie answers, "but I *talk* faster!" He kicks the ball back.

"You talk—too—*much*," Marcus says, and he kicks when he says the word *much*, and the dusty red ball goes flying into the air. A couple of kids cheer.

"I guess maybe I *do*," Stevie says, looking up for the ball. He catches it when he says the word *do*. He narrows his eyes and gets ready to drop-kick the ball one more time.

"So why don't you just shut up for a change?" Marcus yells at him, getting ready to catch the ball—no matter where it lands.

"I guess maybe I *will*," Stevie says, kicking, and the ball flies into the air.

"It's about *time!*" Marcus says, catching it.

Probably things are going to be okay with them and they will be a team again. It's too soon to tell.

Everyone in class enjoyed their one-day vacation from the two bad boys, though. Especially Ms. Marshall, I think, who doesn't know the vacation is over yet. She is sitting back in her chair, breathing like a regular person for once. She pats her braid every so often, like she wants to make sure it is still there.

She catches me looking at her. "Lily, are you finished with your worksheet?" she asks me.

"Almost," I say.

"Huh," Marcus says, sneaking a look at my paper. We are supposed to be matching words and pictures today. I only have one wavy line connecting the word cat with a cat head somebody drew. Case could draw that cat better. *Anyone* could.

"Let's see yours, if you're so great," I whisper to Marcus. Marcus holds up his worksheet. It looks like a giant spider web of connecting lines.

Marcus is so lucky! No fair.

"Lily," Ms. Marshall says, "keep your eyes on your own paper, please. And Marcus, do not bother your neighbor."

I stare down at the paper in front of me. I hate this worksheet! It is so dumb. For question number two, there is a drawing of a dog head. The dog has a collar, and his tongue is hanging way out, and he has big googly eyes. So you could match the drawing up with the words *collar, tongue*, or *eyes*, right? If you could read those words?

But no, the only answer is *dog*. You would be wrong, wrong, wrong if you guessed anything else.

I hate only-answers.

Ms. Marshall has popped up behind me

like a scary jack-in-the-box. *Boi-n-n-ng!* "Lily," she asks, "are you having trouble understanding the assignment?"

"Nuh-uh," I say, shaking my head. I draw a shaky line from the dog head to the word *dog* just to show her that I am not as dumb as she thinks.

Finally, *finally*, the lunch buzzer rings.

When we have finished eating, we all run out onto the playground. The wind is blowing again, and big leaves zip across the yard like they are having a race. The wind makes me want to run and yell!

Stevie and Marcus are whispering together over by the climbing structure.

LaVon and Daisy look shivery, but the wind makes them feel excited, just like me.

"Let's skip!" LaVon says, and so the three of

us hold hands and start skipping across the playground. Everybody gets out of our way.

Step - hop! Step - hop! Step - hop! We are all skipping perfectly, for once. I am in the middle. Each time I hop, it seems like the wind is lifting me a little bit higher. I feel like I could bounce right over the top of Betsy Ross Primary School. I could fly!

I could fly right into my mommy's arms. I would say, *I love you and you love me, no matter what! And maybe you were right about the bad dreams going away someday. In fact, maybe those dreams are over for now!*

LaVon and Daisy have nice warm hands, even though it is cold outside.

Hey, maybe we could just keep on skipping and skipping, forever and ever, amen!

CHAPTER EIGHT
The Plan

Tonight is Halloween, and I am almost ready for LaVon's party.

Mommy has just finished making my costume. I am going to be the tooth fairy! I will wear a sparkly silver skirt over my sweatpants and wings on my shoulders. Mommy had problems with the wings, but she finally got them exactly right.

I will get to wear lipstick and everything.

I will be beautiful!

I don't know yet what Daisy and LaVon are going to be. It's a surprise.

Casey and Ned are going to take us

out trick-or-treating. They will be our bodyguards. I guess we will have to share our candy with them.

But after that, Case will take us to LaVon's house—for the sleep-over! Mommy and I already got her a birthday present. It is an aerobics outfit for her doll. It is so cute! I already unwrapped it two times, just to make sure it was okay. But I was careful, and you can barely tell the paper is ripped.

Mommy called Ned's granny about the sleeping bag, and she said I could borrow it. And then Case checked with Ned, and Ned said I could just *keep* it. He insisted! I guess he doesn't use it anymore.

I am so excited about this party! I have hardly wet my bed at all lately, only two or three times. I guess my nighttime self is starting to get the idea about staying dry.

But I have a plan, just to make sure. When I go to bed at LaVon's house, here is what I will do to keep from having the bad dreams that used to make me wet my bed:

1. I will lie on my back, cross my ankles, and put my hands under my head to keep from rolling over in the night, just like Daisy said. She is usually wrong about stuff, but who knows?

2. I will think happy thoughts about Philadelphia and all the fun I am having here now.

3. I will close my eyes and pretend that Mommy is kissing me good night, just like she always does.

And to make sure I don't wet my bed, I won't drink any water, all night long. Maybe Case is right.

I'll only drink lemonade and stuff like that!

If I do wet my bed—well, it won't be the end of the world, Mommy says. Anyone can have an accident! But she is packing me an extra pair of jammies, just in case.

If *you-know-what* happens, here is the plan: I will change my jammies in the bathroom. Then I will crawl back into my soggy sleeping bag and lie there next to my friends.

And I will wait for the sun to come up.